RAINBOW magic ®

The Dance Fairies

For Saskia Rose Lewis,
with lots of love

Special thanks to
Sue Mongredien

ORCHARD BOOKS
338 Euston Road, London NW1 3BH
Orchard Books Australia
Level 17/207 Kent Street, Sydney, NSW 2000
A Paperback Original

© 2007 Rainbow Magic Limited
Rainbow Magic is a registered trademark
First published in 2007 by Orchard Books
Cover illustrations © Georgie Ripper 2007
Inside illustrations © Orchard Books 2007

A CIP catalogue record for this book is available
from the British Library.

ISBN 978 1 84616 496 5
3 5 7 9 10 8 6 4 2

Printed in Great Britain

Orchard Books is a division of Hachette Children's Books,
an Hachette Livre UK company

www.orchardbooks.co.uk

Saskia
the Salsa
Fairy

by Daisy Meadows

ORCHARD BOOKS

www.rainbowmagic.co.uk

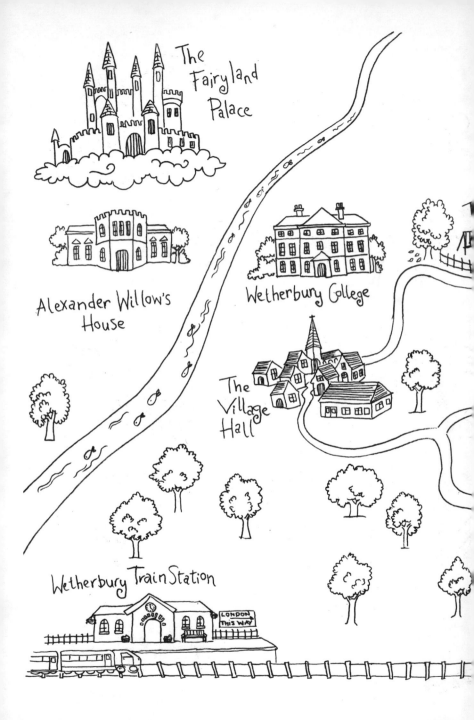

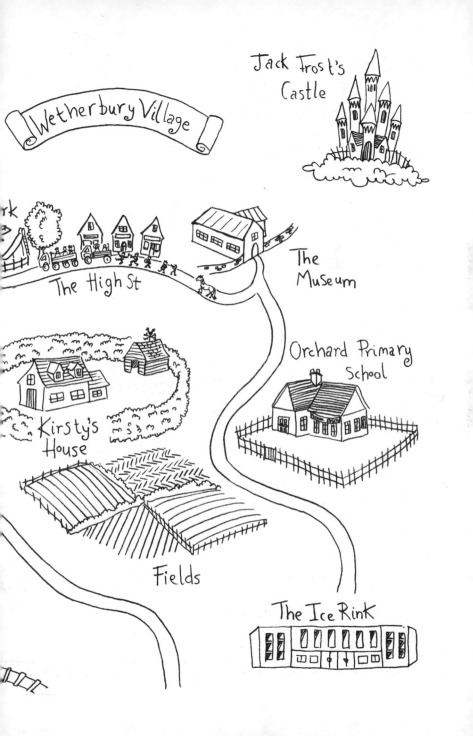

Hold tight to the ribbons, please.
You goblins now may feel a breeze.
I'm summoning a hurricane
To take the ribbons away again.

But, goblins, you'll be swept up too,
For I have work for you to do.
Guard each ribbon carefully,
By using this new power to freeze.

Contents

Fun at the Fiesta   9

The Parade Gets Underway   23

Salsa Slip-ups   31

Goblins Disguised   43

Goblins Give Themselves Away   53

Salsa Success   61

Fun at the Fiesta

"See you later, Mum," Kirsty Tate said, as she and her best friend, Rachel Walker, got ready to leave the house.

"Four o'clock, in front of the Village Hall," Mrs Tate reminded the girls. "I should have finished my work by then. I'm sure you'll have a great time at the fiesta. I can't wait to see all the dancing and costumes. Now, girls, promise me that you'll stick together; it's going to be very busy."

"We will," Kirsty promised. Then, as she and Rachel set off down the road, she added to Rachel, "Of course we'll stick together. Isn't that when we have all our best adventures?"

Rachel grinned. "I hope we have another one today," she replied.

Rachel was staying with Kirsty's family for half-term and the girls were having a very exciting week. A *fairy* exciting week, in fact, because they were helping the Dance Fairies find their missing magical ribbons. The Dance Ribbons helped dancers perform their best throughout Fairyland as well as all around the human world, but Jack Frost, a bad fairy, had stolen the ribbons in order to make sure his goblin servants would dance well at his parties. The Fairy King and Queen had heard about the stolen ribbons, and they'd been to Jack Frost's ice castle to get them back.

Unfortunately, Jack Frost had seen them coming, and he had immediately cast a spell to hurl all the ribbons into the human world, with a goblin to guard each one. While the ribbons were missing, dancing was going wrong in Fairyland and all over the world. Luckily, Kirsty and Rachel had helped the fairies find the Ballet, Disco, Rock 'n' Roll, Tap Dance, and Jazz Ribbons, and these ribbons were now safely back with their rightful fairy owners. There were still two dance ribbons out there somewhere, though, and the girls were keen to track them down.

"The Salsa Ribbon is still lost," Kirsty said, as they walked towards the centre of the village, where the fiesta was taking place. "I wonder if the goblin guarding it will be attracted to the salsa music and turn up at the fiesta today. I hope so."

Rachel was nodding. "If he's anything like the others, having the ribbon will just make him want to  dance, dance, dance," she agreed. "And with all that salsa music playing, I bet he won't be able to resist."

The girls had been surprised at first to see that the goblins who were guarding the dance ribbons could dance really well. In fact, dancing seemed to be the only thing they wanted to do, and any time they heard a tune connected with their particular dance ribbon, they seemed drawn to the music. The fairies had explained to the girls that it was actually the ribbons' magic that made the goblins dance so well. The power

of the dance ribbons was so strong that they made anybody nearby dance wonderfully well – even clumsy goblins!

Kirsty glanced around. "Well, I hope the goblin with the Salsa Ribbon does turn up," she said quietly. "That way we might be able to get the ribbon away from him and safely back to Saskia the Salsa Fairy," she added. "If we don't, the salsa dancing is going to be ruined today!"

At that moment, the girls turned the corner into the high street. For a second, they completely forgot all about goblins as they both took in the sight before them.

The high street looked amazing: colourful banners and streamers had been strung up everywhere, bobbing balloons were pinned to the lampposts, and, lining the street, the girls could see tented pavilions and stalls selling food and drink. Music was playing, everyone was smiling and there seemed to be a great buzz of

excitement in the air.

"This is brilliant!" Rachel said, her eyes shining as she gazed around.

Kirsty grabbed her hand. "Come on," she said eagerly. "Let's go over to the museum, where the parade is going to start. It might be fun to see everyone getting ready."

"OK," Rachel agreed. "And let's keep our eyes open for a goblin!"

As they walked towards the museum, they came across a group of friends gathered around a papier-mâché piñata. The piñata was in the shape of a pineapple and it was dangling from a tree branch. Each person was taking it in turns to put on a blindfold and whack the piñata with a stick, hoping to crack it open and release the goodies inside.

"There's Lucy!" Kirsty said, spotting one of her school friends and waving. Lucy smiled and called them over. "Do you want to have a go?" she asked. "Ooh, yes, please," Kirsty said at once, hurrying up to the piñata. Rachel followed and was given the blindfold to tie around her friend's eyes. Then Rachel and Lucy turned Kirsty around three times before putting the stick in her hand.

Kirsty tottered dizzily towards where she thought the piñata was and bashed it with the stick as hard as she could. *Crack!* The pineapple split open and hundreds of sweets, small toys and glitter tumbled to the ground. Everyone cheered and crowded around to gather up the treats.

Rachel was just about to join them, when she suddenly noticed a tiny spark of light shoot out of the piñata and up into the air. She knew that it couldn't be a sparkly piece of glitter, as it was flying up and not down.

"That's strange!" Rachel said to herself, and then an exciting thought struck her – *Could it be a fairy?*

The Parade Gets Underway

Rachel watched closely as the sparkle zipped over to the side of a pavilion tent. She turned to tell Kirsty but her friend was just pulling off the blindfold and talking to Lucy. Not wanting to lose sight of the sparkle, Rachel raced around the tent for a closer look, her heart thumping. Then she smiled.

It was Saskia the Salsa Fairy! She was perched on the edge of the pavilion roof, waving at Rachel.

Rachel waved back with a grin, just as Kirsty came round the corner with a handful of sweets.

"Do you want some?" Kirsty asked Rachel. "I picked up loads!"

Rachel was too excited to think about sweets. "Look, Kirsty," she whispered, pointing up at the pavilion roof. "Saskia's here!"

Saskia fluttered down towards the girls, and Kirsty saw that she had long black hair, pinned back with a beautiful red rose, and she was wearing a red top and a red skirt with gorgeous orange ruffles.

The girls had met all the Dance Fairies on the very first day of their adventure, so they recognised Saskia right away.

"Hello, Rachel. Hello, Kirsty," the fairy said, smiling as she landed on Kirsty's shoulder. "I'm here to find my ribbon. I've got a strong feeling it's somewhere nearby — and I have to get it back so that all the dancing in the fiesta goes well today."

"We'll help look for it," Kirsty said at once. "We've been keeping an eye out for goblins, but we haven't seen any yet."

"There are going to be lots of salsa dancers in the parade," Rachel added. "The goblin might be attracted to the salsa music and follow them."

Saskia's face brightened. "Let's try and find the goblin before the parade starts," she suggested, "otherwise it might be spoiled."

"Yes, what are we waiting for?" Rachel said determinedly. "Let's get

out there and find that goblin!"

Saskia hid herself behind Kirsty's hair as the girls headed for the start point of the parade. They arrived to find people bustling about, preparing for the parade to begin. Last-minute touches of make-up were being applied, costumes were being smoothed and checked, and the speakers and microphones were being tested.

"It's hard to spot a goblin when everyone's rushing around like this," Rachel said. "And there are so many people here. How are we ever going to find him?"

Saskia was fidgeting on Kirsty's shoulder. "I don't know, but I hope we see him soon," she remarked. "The parade is going to begin any minute!"

The girls scanned the crowds. Leading the parade was a group of women in flamboyant scarlet flamenco dresses and matching scarlet shoes.

The women were accompanied by gleaming white horses, wearing white feathery plumes set in golden headdresses.

"Wow!" Kirsty said, distracted by the sight. "They look amazing!"

Rachel was peering at everyone in search of a tell-tale flash of goblin green. "The goblin definitely isn't around here," she said after a moment or two. "Not unless he's dressed as a horse!"

Just then, a voice came over the loudspeaker. "Welcome, everyone, to the Wetherbury Fiesta. Let the parade begin!"

The girls and Saskia looked at each other in dismay. "We're too late," Rachel said. "It's starting!"

Salsa Slip-ups

Whistles sounded from the crowd, there was a thunderous drum roll from one of the marching bands, and then some pulsing salsa music started up. Despite their worries about the ribbon, Kirsty, Rachel and Saskia couldn't help feeling excited by the lively carnival atmosphere.

"Let's stand here and watch," Rachel suggested. "We might see the goblin going past in the parade."

Saskia nodded. "I hope so!" she said. "We'll have to watch out for anyone who's dancing especially well. It might be because the ribbon is close to them."

The flamenco dancers waved and blew kisses to the crowd and then led their horses down the street, shaking tambourines, and swishing their skirts

as they paraded along.

People were clapping and cheering
enthusiastically as the horses trotted
by, their white coats glinting in the
sunshine and their feathery headdresses
fluttering in the wind. After them came
the Scintillating Samba Band, the
musicians playing drums, trumpets and
maracas as they marched along in
black trousers with ruffled white shirts.

"This is wonderful!" beamed Saskia,

clapping along in time to the music. "And so far everyone's been walking, rather than dancing, so nothing's gone wrong."

"Ooh, look, she goes to my school!" Kirsty said excitedly, as a salsa dance class full of young people followed after the samba band. She waved at a girl in a blue dress who was twirling around with a partner. "Oops," Kirsty said, as the girl saw Kirsty, waved back and then promptly collided with her partner. "Oh, no," Rachel said in dismay as she saw another girl from the dance class trip over. "It looks like the dancing is beginning to go wrong."

Saskia watched anxiously. "If only I had my ribbon," she sighed, "I could have stopped this from happening!"

Next came a group of salsa dancers, shimmying their way along the parade route. A woman in a long red evening dress danced at the front, carrying a sign that read 'Cuban Break Salsa Group' – and she was just waving it above her head and smiling to the crowd when, suddenly, she stumbled awkwardly on her high heels, dropped the sign and almost fell over.

Saskia winced. "We've got to find my ribbon before someone hurts themselves," she said. "Where is that goblin?"

"I don't know," Rachel replied, as one of the salsa dancers accidentally trod on his partner's toe. "Ouch!" she exclaimed sympathetically.

The Cuban Break Salsa Group passed by, to be followed by a float. There were a lot of oohs and ahhhs from the crowd as it moved past, because the whole platform had been set up to look like an exotic garden paradise, with palm trees and fabulous painted scenery making the whole float a riot of colourful flowers, birds and butterflies. The salsa dancers on the float were wearing fantastic costumes to make themselves look like tropical birds, and they were performing some very complicated salsa dance moves. It wasn't long before the crowds lining the street were applauding and cheering in approval.

"Those salsa dancers are really good!"
Saskia said. "What's going on?

Kirsty grinned. "I've got a feeling
your ribbon must be on that float with
them, Saskia," she suggested.

"I bet you're right, Kirsty!" the little
fairy agreed.

"Let's follow the float!" Rachel
suggested eagerly.

Kirsty glanced around as the float
moved past and her face fell. "It's going

to be tricky," she said. "There are so many people here! We're really going to have to fight to get through the crowds."

Saskia smiled. "Ah, but why walk, when you can fly?" she asked cheerfully. "Let's find somewhere quiet for me to work some fairy magic."

Kirsty and Rachel managed to squeeze their way through the crowd to an empty side street, and then Saskia waved her wand over them. With a swirl of fiery orange sparkles, Kirsty and Rachel

were immediately transformed into
tiny fairies.

Kirsty flapped her delicate wings
happily, loving the way that they
shimmered in the afternoon sunshine.

"Now we can get really close to the
float and have a better look at the
dancers," Rachel suggested, as the three
friends fluttered high above the crowds.

"Good idea," Saskia agreed, "but we'll have to be very careful not to be spotted."

Quick as a flash, the three fairies zoomed down to the float and hid behind one of the palm trees. "Right, keep your eyes peeled for the goblin," Kirsty whispered, peeping out from behind a palm leaf. "He must be here somewhere, and the sooner we spot him, the better!"

Goblins Disguised

The three fairies gazed around at the
dancers, studying them carefully, but
it wasn't easy to make out their faces.
The costumed dancers were whirling
around so fast, they seemed more like
colourful blurs than real people.

"I can't believe they can dance
so quickly on a moving float!"

Kirsty marvelled.

Saskia nodded. "Which makes me even more sure that the Salsa Ribbon must be here, helping them keep their balance," she said.

Just then, Rachel spotted two rather short dancers in the middle of the float. They were both dancing exceptionally well. One was dressed as a parrot and the other as a bird of paradise with a spectacular,

rainbow-coloured feathery tail. Both dancers had wings attached to their arms, and beaks fastened over their noses with elastic. "Look!" Rachel hissed, pointing the short dancers out to Saskia and Kirsty. "Those two are the best dancers of all."

The three fairies watched as the parrot took the bird of paradise's hand and the bird of paradise danced a little turn under the parrot's outstretched wing.

"Nice," Saskia said approvingly.
"That's called an Alemana Turn," she
told the girls. Then she stared at the
dancers, hard. "They're very small,
aren't they?"

"Perhaps they're goblins!"
Kirsty hissed.

The three fairies looked at one
another in dismay. Two goblins? One

was bad enough,
but having two
to outwit was
surely going
to be double
trouble.
"At least
only one of them
will have the freezing
power," Kirsty said, trying to be

positive, but she couldn't help a little shiver. Before sending the goblins into the human world to guard the Dance Fairies' ribbons, Jack Frost had given them each the power to freeze things. But the girls knew that the magic only lasted for as long as the goblin had a magic ribbon in his possession.

The three friends zoomed a little nearer to the dancing goblins, hoping to spot Saskia's orange ribbon. They zipped between dancers really quickly, so that they wouldn't be spotted by anyone in the crowd or on the float.

47

Eventually, they reached a palm tree near the spot where the goblins were dancing, and perched on one of its big leaves for a closer look.

Suddenly, Saskia let out an excited squeak and pointed at the bird of paradise's feathery tail.

There among his feathers was a long, fiery orange ribbon. The Salsa Ribbon!

"I'll get it," Kirsty offered, and she made a dive for the

bird of paradise's tail. She was just
about to grab the ribbon, when the
other goblin noticed her over his friend's
shoulder. With a yell of surprise he
yanked his friend towards him, hastily
twirling the bird of paradise under his
arm so that the feathery tail was out of
Kirsty's reach.

The two goblins lifted up
their beaks and pulled
rude faces at
Kirsty, Rachel
and Saskia.
Rachel gasped in
recognition as she
noticed the parrot
goblin's very pointy nose.
He was the same goblin who'd been
guarding Jessica the Jazz Fairy's ribbon,

which they'd only got back yesterday!

The pointy-nosed goblin glared at them. It was clear that he recognised the girls, too. "We'll have to get away from those pesky fairies," Rachel heard him warn his friend. "They're after your Salsa Ribbon!"

And then, before Kirsty, Rachel or Saskia could move, he'd grabbed the other goblin's hand and together they took a running jump off the slow-moving float.

The three fairy friends could only watch, open-mouthed, as the goblins opened up their feathery arms and glided to the ground before racing off through the crowd towards the nearby park.

"After them!" cried Rachel.

Goblins Give Themselves Away

As Kirsty zoomed off in pursuit, she noticed that a few people in the crowd were staring after the running birds in confusion. Fortunately, though, they soon turned back to the parade. Meanwhile, Kirsty, Rachel and Saskia flew after the goblins as fast as they could, making sure they all kept high

up in the air so that they were out
of sight.

The goblins had run through the park
gates and were now
dashing across one
of the lawns at
top speed. They
seemed to be
making for a small
wooded area at the
back of the park, and Kirsty, Rachel
and Saskia could hear them yelling to
each other in panicked voices.

"Where can we hide? Where shall we
go?" the parrot goblin shouted.

"Birds live in trees, don't they?" the
goblin with the ribbon replied. "Let's
hide in a tree – nobody will notice
us there!"

The parrot goblin seemed to think this was a very good idea, because he immediately began scrambling up the nearest tree trunk. The bird of paradise goblin clambered awkwardly after him, his colourful tail dragging through the autumn leaves on the branches as he did so.

Moments later, Kirsty, Rachel and Saskia arrived at the base of the tree. Up through the gold, brown and orange leaves, they could see the

goblins huddling together on one of the branches. "They'll never find us now," the parrot goblin's voice floated down. "Thanks to my brilliant idea!"

"We're masters of disguise!" agreed the bird of paradise goblin happily. "Invisible to the rest of the world!"

"I quite like this bird malarkey," the parrot goblin said. "Listen to this. *Cheep! Cheep!*"

Rachel watched as the bird of paradise goblin elbowed his chirruping friend. "Parrots don't cheep," he hissed. "They squawk, and say funny things."

Kirsty saw the parrot goblin scratch his head. "Er...pieces of eight!" he screeched. "Pieces of eight! Who's a pretty boy, then?"

Rachel, Kirsty and Saskia all looked at one another and couldn't help giggling. The goblins weren't well

disguised at all. Their bright costumes stood out against the autumn leaves and they were much, much bigger than real birds.

"Nobody would be convinced by that parrot impression," Kirsty laughed.

"'Masters of disguise' indeed..." Rachel chuckled to herself, and then a thought struck her. "You know, those goblins have given me an idea." She turned to Saskia. "Saskia, could you use your magic to camouflage Kirsty and me, so that we blend in with the leaves of the tree? If we're disguised, we might be able to sneak up on the goblins and grab the Salsa Ribbon!"

Saskia nodded. "That's a great idea,"  she said and waved her wand over the girls. A stream of glittering orange sparkles poured from the tip of her wand and fizzed around Rachel and Kirsty.

As the mist of sparkles cleared, Rachel grinned to see that she and Kirsty were now wearing wonderful little outfits made from autumnal leaves. "Your hair's still dark, though," she said to Kirsty, noticing how it stood out against the russet colours of Kirsty's outfit. "I wonder…"

But Saskia was already waving her wand again and another swirl of magical sparkles surrounded the girls. Kirsty and Rachel gasped as they saw each other's skin and hair turn orange, too.

"Perfect!" laughed Kirsty. "Now, let's get that Salsa Ribbon!"

Salsa Success

Rachel and Kirsty fluttered silently up the tree and perched on a branch just below the goblins. The goblins were getting rather carried away with their bird noises, and it was all Kirsty could do not to burst out laughing as she listened to the terrible din.

"*Tweet! Tweet! Tweet!*" twittered the

bird of paradise goblin. "*La-la-la-la-la!*"

"What's that all about then?" the parrot goblin demanded. "What's with the la-la-las?" The other goblin looked indignant. "I'm a songbird, aren't I?" he replied. "That's just one of my songs!"

"What, la-la-la?" the parrot goblin asked, looking disbelieving. "Real birds don't sing la-la-la!"

"I'm just getting into it, aren't I?" his friend said sulkily. "How about this? *Coo, coo, cooo!*"

"You're not a pigeon!" the parrot goblin snapped. "Look, you either do this properly or not at all!"

Rachel didn't dare look at Kirsty as the goblins started bickering heatedly about their bird noises. She knew she'd only burst out laughing if she caught Kirsty's eye! The goblins seemed to have forgotten all about keeping themselves hidden; their voices were getting louder and louder as they argued.

Rachel edged stealthily along the branch towards the bird of paradise goblin's tail. She pressed herself against

a twig, waiting for the right moment
to strike and then, as the two goblins
began arguing about who had the best
costume, she darted forwards and deftly
plucked the orange ribbon from the
goblin's feathery tail.

Kirsty grabbed hold of it too and the
two brave fairies flew away from the
tree, carrying the ribbon between them.

As it trailed through the air behind
them, they suddenly heard the
parrot goblin let out a great squawk
of shock.

"Look! Those leaves are making off
with our ribbon!"
he cried in
amazement.

His friend
stared after
them. "They're
not leaves.
They're pesky
fairies! But they've
gone orange!"

"Well, I'm not letting them get away
with this!" the parrot goblin declared,
and then he made a frantic lunge for
Kirsty and Rachel.

"Careful!" yelled the bird of paradise goblin as the parrot goblin bumped into him. And then both goblins lost their balance and tumbled out of the tree. Luckily, they landed on a big pile of autumn leaves.

The goblins leapt to their feet, looking furious, but Saskia was pointing her wand at them threateningly.

"It's time for you two to go,"

she said firmly, "or I'll turn *you* orange! And who ever heard of an orange goblin?" The parrot goblin pulled off his beak and threw it down sullenly. "This is your fault," he fumed to his friend. "If you hadn't been doing your la-la-las so loud, they never would have found us up there!" "My fault!" the other goblin retorted. "What about you and your parrot screeches?"

Rachel and Kirsty hovered in the air
and smiled at each
other as the
goblins
stomped
away crossly,
still moaning.
"Those goblins
won't be causing
any more problems for the fiesta, thank
goodness!" Rachel said happily.

"Here you are, Saskia," Kirsty said
as they handed the Salsa Ribbon over
to her.

Saskia waved her wand over the
ribbon, shrinking it to its Fairyland size
and then reattached it to her wand
with a happy smile. The ribbon shone
a deep, warm orange in the sunshine,

and fairy sparkles rippled up and down
its length. "Thank you, girls," she said.
"I'm so pleased to have my ribbon
back. Now all the salsa dancing will be
as good as ever!"

She waved her wand at Kirsty and
Rachel and turned them both back into
girls, with their normal skin, hair and
clothes. "There," she said. "Now you're
all ready to enjoy the rest of the fiesta."

"Thanks, Saskia,"
Rachel said.
"We will."

The girls said
goodbye to the
little fairy and she
zoomed away in
a last flash of
orange sparkles.

"It's nearly time to meet Mum," Kirsty said, glancing at her watch. "But first I want to see what else is in the parade, and I really fancy doing some dancing myself!"

She and Rachel made their way back to the high street where the crowds were still clapping and cheering the dancers in the parade.

The girls were pleased to see that none of the dancers seemed to be having any trouble now – in fact, they all seemed to be dancing brilliantly, and the audience was dancing and clapping in time to the salsa music.

"Everyone's having a great time," Rachel said, smiling as she joined in the dancing. "What a brilliant day!"

Kirsty nodded, twirling around on the spot. "And who knows? Tomorrow might be even better," she said excitedly. "After all, there's only one more magic ribbon left to find!"

The Dance Fairies

Saskia the Salsa Fairy has got
her magic ribbon back. Now Rachel
and Kirsty must help

Imogen the Ice Dance Fairy

BETHANY
THE BALLET FAIRY
978-1-84616-490-3

JADE
THE DISCO FAIRY
978-1-84616-491-0

REBECCA
THE ROCK 'N' ROLL FAIRY
978-1-84616-492-7

TASHA
THE TAP DANCE FAIRY
978-1-84616-493-4

JESSICA
THE JAZZ FAIRY
978-1-84616-495-8

SASKIA
THE SALSA FAIRY
978-1-84616-496-5

IMOGEN
THE ICE DANCE FAIRY
978-1-84616-497-2

Win Rainbow Magic goodies!

In every book in the Rainbow Magic Dance Fairies series (books 50-56) there is a hidden picture of a ribbon with a secret letter in it. Find all seven letters and re-arrange them to make a special Dance Fairies word, then send it to us. Each month we will put the entries into a draw and select one winner to receive a Rainbow Magic Sparkly T-shirt and Goody Bag!

Send your entry on a postcard to Rainbow Magic Dance Fairies Competition, Orchard Books, 338 Euston Road, London NW1 3BH.
Australian readers should write to Hachette Children's Books, Level 17/207 Kent Street, Sydney, NSW 2000.
New Zealand readers should write to Rainbow Magic Competition, 4 Whetu Place, Mairangi Bay, Auckland, NZ. Don't forget to include your name and address. Only one entry per child.
Final draw: 30th September 2008.

Good luck!

Have you checked out the

website at:
www.rainbowmagic.co.uk

by Daisy Meadows

The Rainbow Fairies

Ruby the Red Fairy	ISBN	978 1 84362 016 7
Amber the Orange Fairy	ISBN	978 1 84362 017 4
Saffron the Yellow Fairy	ISBN	978 1 84362 018 1
Fern the Green Fairy	ISBN	978 1 84362 019 8
Sky the Blue Fairy	ISBN	978 1 84362 020 4
Izzy the Indigo Fairy	ISBN	978 1 84362 021 1
Heather the Violet Fairy	ISBN	978 1 84362 022 8

The Weather Fairies

Crystal the Snow Fairy	ISBN	978 1 84362 633 6
Abigail the Breeze Fairy	ISBN	978 1 84362 634 3
Pearl the Cloud Fairy	ISBN	978 1 84362 635 0
Goldie the Sunshine Fairy	ISBN	978 1 84362 636 7
Evie the Mist Fairy	ISBN	978 1 84362 637 4
Storm the Lightning Fairy	ISBN	978 1 84362 638 1
Hayley the Rain Fairy	ISBN	978 1 84362 641 1

The Party Fairies

Cherry the Cake Fairy	ISBN	978 1 84362 818 7
Melodie the Music Fairy	ISBN	978 1 84362 819 4
Grace the Glitter Fairy	ISBN	978 1 84362 820 0
Honey the Sweet Fairy	ISBN	978 1 84362 821 7
Polly the Party Fun Fairy	ISBN	978 184362 822 4
Phoebe the Fashion Fairy	ISBN	978 1 84362 823 1
Jasmine the Present Fairy	ISBN	978 1 84362 824 8

The Jewel Fairies

India the Moonstone Fairy	ISBN	978 1 84362 958 0
Scarlett the Garnet Fairy	ISBN	978 1 84362 954 2
Emily the Emerald Fairy	ISBN	978 1 84362 955 9
Chloe the Topaz Fairy	ISBN	978 1 84362 956 6
Amy the Amethyst Fairy	ISBN	978 1 84362 957 3
Sophie the Sapphire Fairy	ISBN	978 1 84362 953 5
Lucy the Diamond Fairy	ISBN	978 1 84362 959 7

The Pet Keeper Fairies

Katie the Kitten Fairy	ISBN	978 1 84616 166 7
Bella the Bunny Fairy	ISBN	978 1 84616 170 4
Georgia the Guinea Pig Fairy	ISBN	978 1 84616 168 1
Lauren the Puppy Fairy	ISBN	978 1 84616 169 8
Harriet the Hamster Fairy	ISBN	978 1 84616 167 4
Molly the Goldfish Fairy	ISBN	978 1 84616 172 8
Penny the Pony Fairy	ISBN	978 1 84616 171 1

The Fun Day Fairies

Megan the Monday Fairy	ISBN	978 184616 188 9
Tallulah the Tuesday Fairy	ISBN	978 1 84616 189 6
Willow the Wednesday Fairy	ISBN	978 1 84616 190 2
Thea the Thursday Fairy	ISBN	978 1 84616 191 9
Freya the Friday Fairy	ISBN	978 1 84616 192 6
Sienna the Saturday Fairy	ISBN	978 1 84616 193 3
Sarah the Sunday Fairy	ISBN	978 1 84616 194 0

The Petal Fairies

Tia the Tulip Fairy	ISBN	978 1 84616 457 6
Pippa the Poppy Fairy	ISBN	978 1 84616 458 3
Louise the Lily Fairy	ISBN	978 1 84616 459 0
Charlotte the Sunflower Fairy	ISBN	978 1 84616 460 6
Olivia the Orchid Fairy	ISBN	978 1 84616 461 3
Danielle the Daisy Fairy	ISBN	978 1 84616 462 0
Ella the Rose Fairy	ISBN	978 1 84616 464 4

The Dance Fairies

Bethany the Ballet Fairy	ISBN	978 1 84616 490 3
Jade the Disco Fairy	ISBN	978 1 84616 491 0
Rebecca the Rock'n'Roll Fairy	ISBN	978 1 84616 492 7
Tasha the Tap Dance Fairy	ISBN	978 1 84616 493 4
Jessica the Jazz Fairy	ISBN	978 1 84616 495 8
Saskia the Salsa Fairy	ISBN	978 1 84616 496 5
Imogen the Ice Dance Fairy	ISBN	978 1 84616 497 2

Holly the Christmas Fairy	ISBN	978 1 84362 661 9
Summer the Holiday Fairy	ISBN	978 1 84362 960 3
Stella the Star Fairy	ISBN	978 1 84362 869 9
Kylie the Carnival Fairy	ISBN	978 1 84616 175 9
Paige the Pantomime Fairy	ISBN	978 1 84616 209 1
Flora the Fancy Dress Fairy	ISBN	978 1 84616 505 4

The Rainbow Magic Treasury	ISBN	978 1 84616 047 9
Fairy Fashion Dress-Up Book	ISBN	978 1 84616 371 5
Fairy Friends Sticker Book	ISBN	978 1 84616 370 8
Fairy Stencils Sticker Colouring Book		978 1 84616 476 7
Fairy Style Fashion Sticker Book		978 1 84616 478 1

Coming soon:

| Chrissie the Wish Fairy | ISBN | 978 1 84616 506 1 |

All priced at £3.99.
Holly the Christmas Fairy, Summer the Holiday Fairy, Stella the Star Fairy,
Kylie the Carnival Fairy, Paige the Pantomime Fairy, Flora the Fancy Dress Fairy and
Chrissie the Wish Fairy are priced at £5.99. *The Rainbow Magic Treasury* is priced at £12.99.
Rainbow Magic books are available from all good bookshops, or can be ordered
direct from the publisher: Orchard Books, PO BOX 29, Douglas IM99 1BQ
Credit card orders please telephone 01624 836000
or fax 01624 837033 or visit our Internet site: www.orchardbooks.co.uk
or e-mail: bookshop@enterprise.net for details.

To order please quote title, author and ISBN and your full name and address.
Cheques and postal orders should be made payable to 'Bookpost plc.'
Postage and packing is FREE within the UK
(overseas customers should add £2.00 per book).
Prices and availability are subject to change.

Look out for the Sporty Fairies!

NAOMI
THE NETBALL FAIRY
978-1-84616-891-8

ZOE
THE ROLLERBLADING FAIRY
978-1-84616-890-1

FRANCESCA
THE FOOTBALL FAIRY
978-1-84616-889-5

HELENA
THE HORSERIDING FAIRY
978-1-84616-888-8

GEMMA
THE GYMNASTICS FAIRY
978-1-84616-894-9

ALICE
THE TENNIS FAIRY
978-1-84616-893-2

SAMANTHA
THE SWIMMING FAIRY
978-1-84616-892-5

Available
April 2008